<u>Upcoming Book</u>
<u>Harlie Doodle Dog.</u>
<u>Making Better Choices Series</u>

Harlie Doodle Dog: My New School

Harlie Doodle Dog: Time for Bed

Harlie Doodle Dog: Learns to Wait

Harlie Doodle Dog: Makes New Friends

Harlie Doodle Dog: Family Rules

Harlie Doodle Learning
Making Better Choices Series

To my mom, dad and sister, for being my biggest cheerleaders!
Love you so much. K.

Find Your Calm

10 9 8 7 6
5 4 3 2 1

Story by Karina Bossé

Harlie Doodle Learning
Making Better Choices Series

Harlie Doodle is a dog,
Who's cuddly, soft, and sweet.

He likes to play with dinosaurs,
And stomp things with their feet.

But that sweet Harlie Doodle,
Is stubborn every day!

And when he's feeling angry,
He throws his toys away!

"Harlie, you are fuming!"
Mommy said to him one day.

"Let's find a way to calm you down,
So you can go and play."

Mommy had a great idea,
And went to fetch a chart.

"Here's some ways to find
your calm,
Let's practice from the
start."

Harlie saw the pictures.
They were things that he could do!
So many ways to calm his mind,
His heart and body too.

Harlie's
Calm Down Strategies

Take deep breaths

Count back from 10 to 1

Hug your knees

Read a book

Balance on 1 foot

Take a sip of water

Think happy thoughts

You can take some deep
breaths,
And then you count to ten.

You inhale slow... then exhale slow,
Then do it all again.

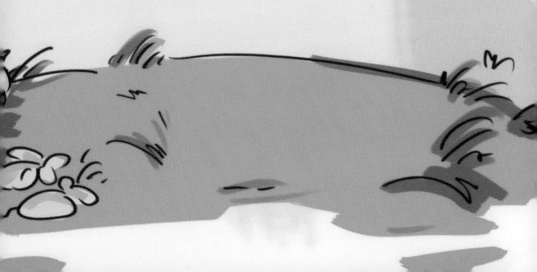

Counting is a great way,
To calm the body and the
mind.

Count back from ten to one,
Now you're ready to be kind.

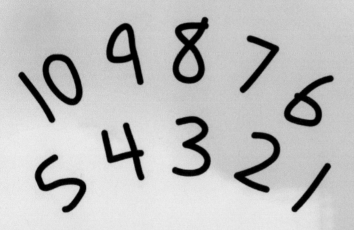

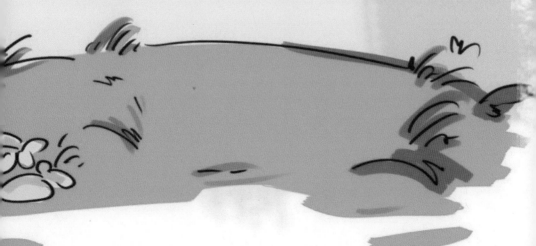

Can you try to hug yourself?
Wrap your arms around your
knees.
Slowly count
to the number ten,
Or sing your ABCs.

Sometimes peace and
quiet,
Can also calm your
heart.
Let's sit and read a
book,
About a pup named
Lemontart.

Can you balance on
one foot?
Harlie tried but
hopped around.

He yipped and yapped
every time,
His paw would touch
the ground.

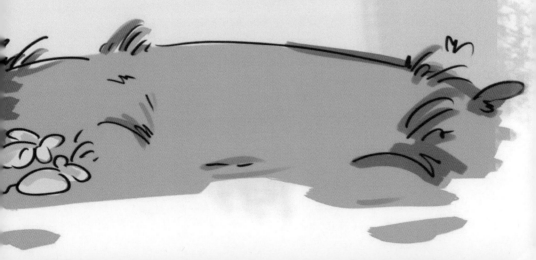

Drinking water can
also help,
So they took some
little sips.

Harlie's anger had almost cooled. He giggled with happy yips.

Time for some joyful thoughts!
Imagine a happy place.

Now Harlie was ready
to go and play,
With a smile upon his
face.

Parent Tips

- review the visual schedule (picture list) with your child before you begin to use it

- practice each calming strategy

- as you are practicing, talk to your child about what they feel in their body

- role-play situations that would make your child mad, and then pick a calming strategy to use

- ask them to pick one or two strategies that they think they would use when angry and get them to circle those strategies on the chart

- have copies of the chart handy and when your child becomes frustrated or mad, show the chart, simply say "find your calm" and point to one of the strategies they previously chose

- help them move through the calming strategy, such as count backwards with them

Harlie Doodle Learning
Making Better Choices Series

Harlie's Calm Down Strategies

Take deep breaths

Count back from 10 to 1

Hug your knees

Read a book

Balance on 1 foot

Take a sip of water

Think happy thoughts

Follow my Facebook Page for updates on upcoming books, contests and fun facts!

Karina Bosse, author of Harlie Doodle Dog: Making Better Choices Series

Author

Printed in Great Britain
by Amazon

34115891R00021